the Pagemaster

This storybook belongs to:

Joey Anthony Sanchez

LOOK TO THE BOOKS

Based on the screenplay by
David Kirschner, David Casci, and Ernie Contreras,
from the David Kirschner and David Casci story.

Published by Bedrock Press
An imprint of Turner Publishing, Inc.
A Subsidiary of Turner Broadcasting System, Inc.
1050 Techwood Drive, N.W.
Atlanta, Georgia 30318

First Edition 10 9 8 7 6 5 4 3 2 1
ISBN: 1-57036-098-7

Distributed by Andrews and McMeel
A Universal Press Syndicate Company
4900 Main Street
Kansas City, MO 64112

Illustrated by DiCicco Digital Arts with Len Smith
Printed and bound by Lake Book, Chicago

the Pagemaster
STORYBOOK

Bedrock Press

Atlanta

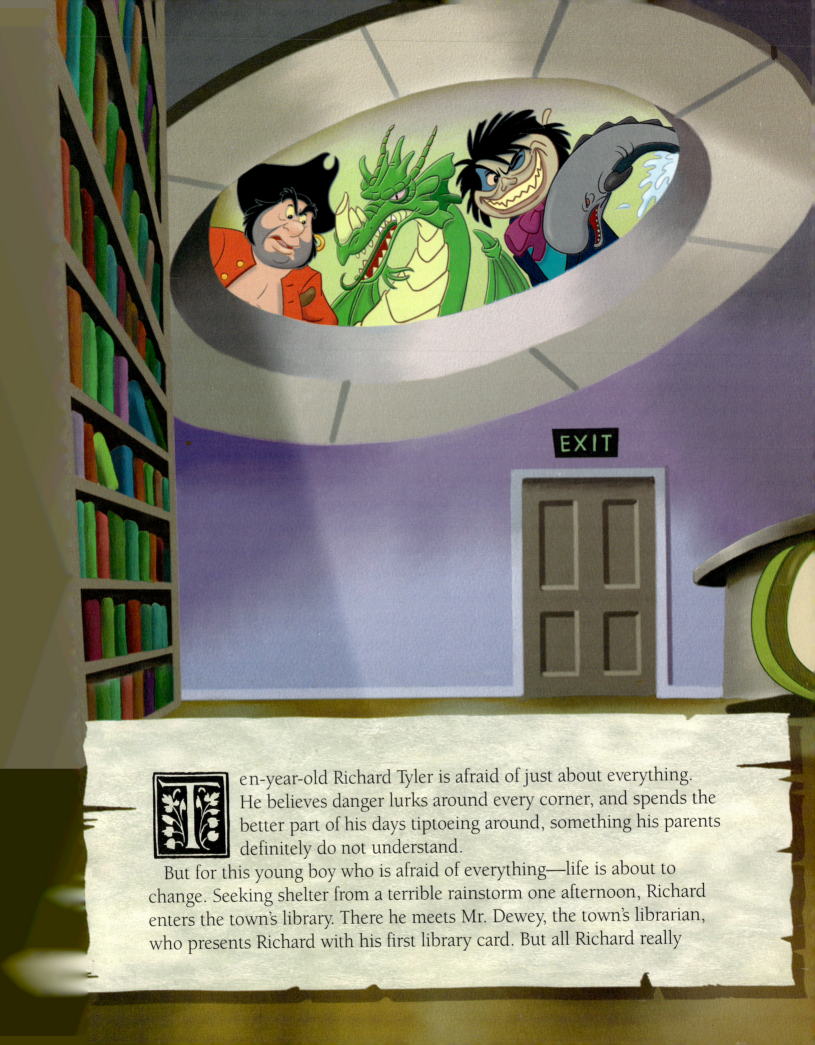

Ten-year-old Richard Tyler is afraid of just about everything. He believes danger lurks around every corner, and spends the better part of his days tiptoeing around, something his parents definitely do not understand.

But for this young boy who is afraid of everything—life is about to change. Seeking shelter from a terrible rainstorm one afternoon, Richard enters the town's library. There he meets Mr. Dewey, the town's librarian, who presents Richard with his first library card. But all Richard really

wants is to find the way out. Disappointed, Mr. Dewey points to the glowing green EXIT sign across the library. Richard begins to make his way toward the exit, but stops in the great, round hall to look at a mural painted on the high ceiling. It is magnificent! And weird. There are pictures of odd-looking people and creatures, and one wizened old man. Looking up at the mural, Richard leans a little too far back, and **CRASH!** He falls onto the shiny marble floor. Everything goes dark. And this is where Richard's story begins.

When he awoke, Richard felt a tinge of fear. He stood up cautiously. "H-hello?" he called out. Looking around, he thought everything in the library seemed to be the same, but somehow everything was different, too.

Now, what could it possibly . . . ?

"I-I'm a . . . cartoon!" he cried, looking at his hands.

"More precisely, you are an illustration," came a deep and smooth voice from the shadows. An old man stepped into view.

"W-who are you?" asked Richard, gulping back his terror.

"I am the Pagemaster," the bearded old man said. "Keeper of the books and guardian of the written word."

Richard looked at the ceiling. "You're the guy from up there!" he cried. He looked suspiciously about the room. "Where're the others?"

"Why, they're here, of course, and all around," said the Pagemaster, pointing to the rows and rows of bookshelves.

"M-maybe you could show me the way out?" asked Richard, trembling.

"If it's what you truly want," said the Pagemaster. When Richard nodded nervously, the old man cried, "Splendid!" and motioned for Richard to follow him.

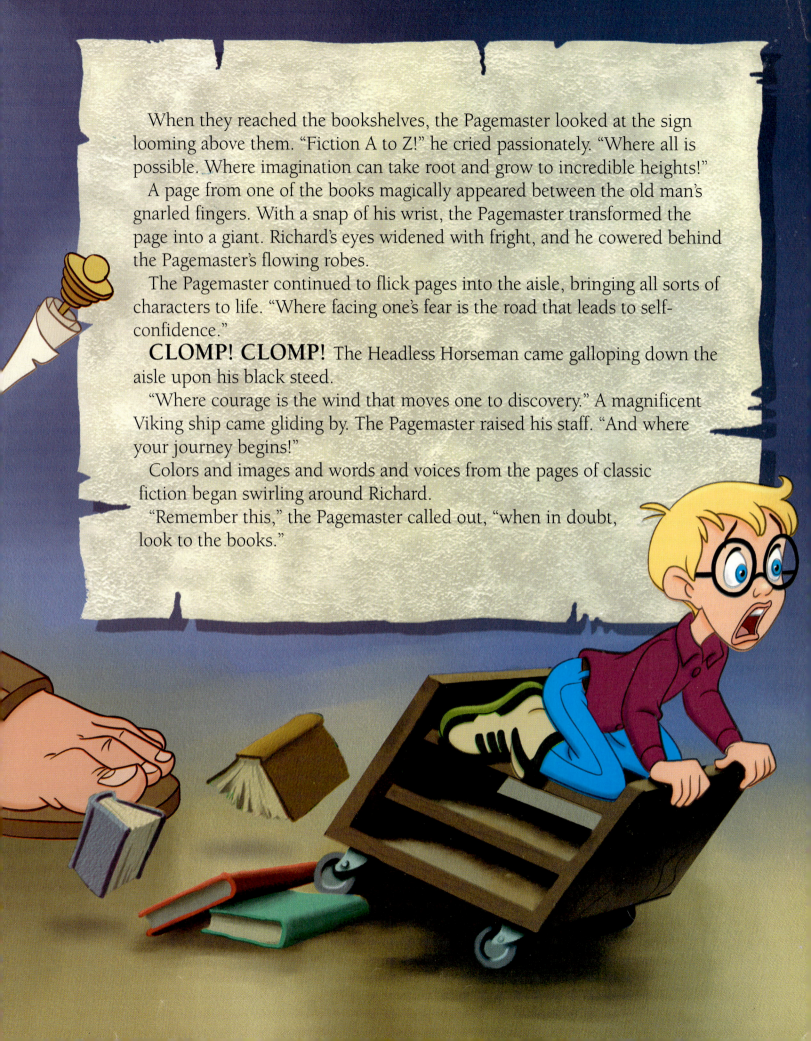

When they reached the bookshelves, the Pagemaster looked at the sign looming above them. "Fiction A to Z!" he cried passionately. "Where all is possible. Where imagination can take root and grow to incredible heights!"

A page from one of the books magically appeared between the old man's gnarled fingers. With a snap of his wrist, the Pagemaster transformed the page into a giant. Richard's eyes widened with fright, and he cowered behind the Pagemaster's flowing robes.

The Pagemaster continued to flick pages into the aisle, bringing all sorts of characters to life. "Where facing one's fear is the road that leads to self-confidence."

CLOMP! CLOMP! The Headless Horseman came galloping down the aisle upon his black steed.

"Where courage is the wind that moves one to discovery." A magnificent Viking ship came gliding by. The Pagemaster raised his staff. "And where your journey begins!"

Colors and images and words and voices from the pages of classic fiction began swirling around Richard.

"Remember this," the Pagemaster called out, "when in doubt, look to the books."

The next thing Richard knew, he was on top of a bookcart being swept down the aisle of the Fiction section. He held on tight as the bookcart raced through the aisle—faster and faster! The bookcart slammed into a phone booth, sending Richard flying to the floor and scattering books everywhere.

As Richard sat up, he could see that a pile of books nearby was beginning to move! Up popped a strange-looking book from underneath the rubble. It scrambled to the top of the pile, with a sword in one hand and a hook for the other. "Where's the son of a rum puncheon knocked the wind from me sails?" growled the scrappy old book.

Richard gasped. The book spun around, ruffling its pages, and pointed its sword right at Richard. "You fiction 'er nonfiction?"

"I'm R-R-Richard T-Tyler."

"What kind of book would that be?" he asked suspiciously.

Richard couldn't believe he was talking to a book. "I-I'm not a book." He pulled out his library card. "See? Here's my name."

The book examined the card closely, then lifted his eye patch. "A library card!" he exclaimed. "Beggin' yer pardon, lad. Didn't know ye was a customer. Name's Adventure, matey. At yer service."

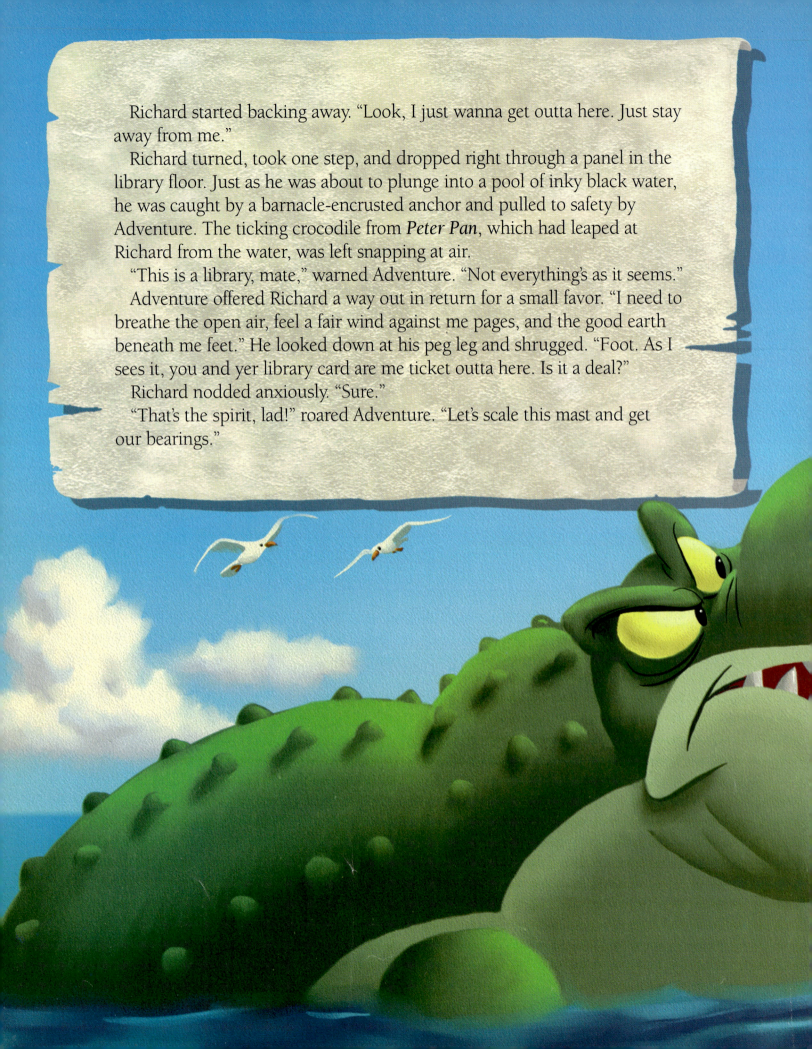

Richard started backing away. "Look, I just wanna get outta here. Just stay away from me."

Richard turned, took one step, and dropped right through a panel in the library floor. Just as he was about to plunge into a pool of inky black water, he was caught by a barnacle-encrusted anchor and pulled to safety by Adventure. The ticking crocodile from *Peter Pan*, which had leaped at Richard from the water, was left snapping at air.

"This is a library, mate," warned Adventure. "Not everything's as it seems."

Adventure offered Richard a way out in return for a small favor. "I need to breathe the open air, feel a fair wind against me pages, and the good earth beneath me feet." He looked down at his peg leg and shrugged. "Foot. As I sees it, you and yer library card are me ticket outta here. Is it a deal?"

Richard nodded anxiously. "Sure."

"That's the spirit, lad!" roared Adventure. "Let's scale this mast and get our bearings."

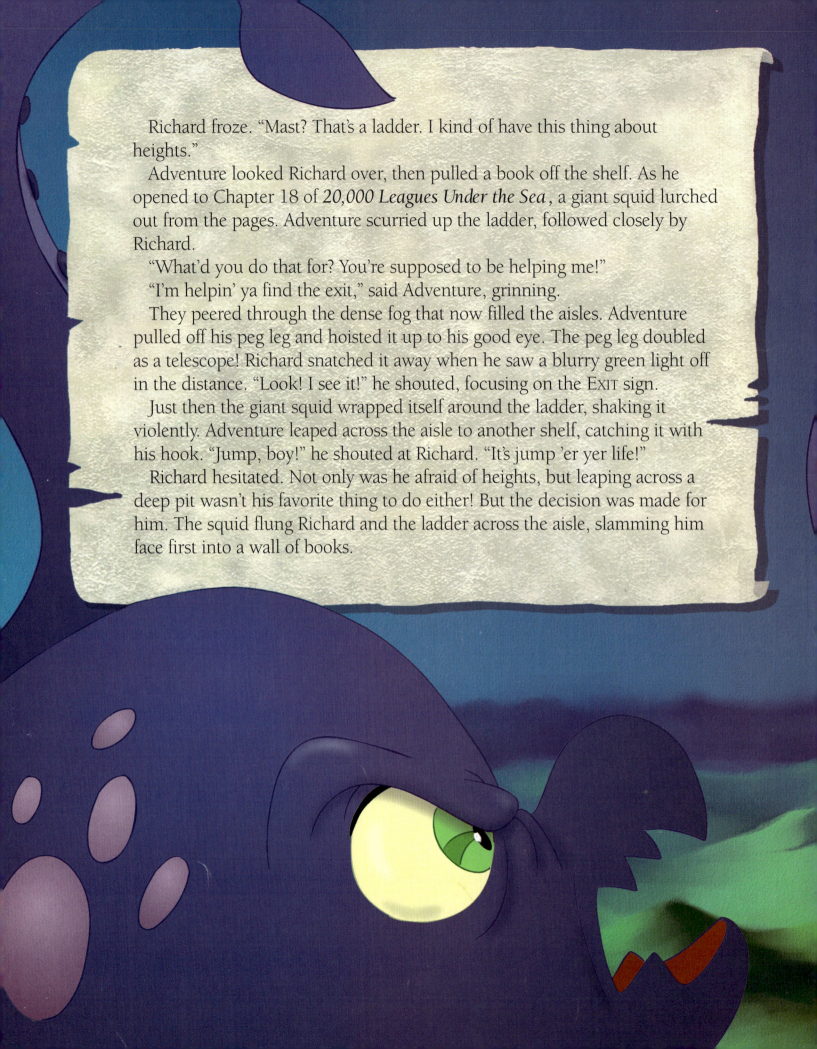

Richard froze. "Mast? That's a ladder. I kind of have this thing about heights."

Adventure looked Richard over, then pulled a book off the shelf. As he opened to Chapter 18 of *20,000 Leagues Under the Sea*, a giant squid lurched out from the pages. Adventure scurried up the ladder, followed closely by Richard.

"What'd you do that for? You're supposed to be helping me!"

"I'm helpin' ya find the exit," said Adventure, grinning.

They peered through the dense fog that now filled the aisles. Adventure pulled off his peg leg and hoisted it up to his good eye. The peg leg doubled as a telescope! Richard snatched it away when he saw a blurry green light off in the distance. "Look! I see it!" he shouted, focusing on the EXIT sign.

Just then the giant squid wrapped itself around the ladder, shaking it violently. Adventure leaped across the aisle to another shelf, catching it with his hook. "Jump, boy!" he shouted at Richard. "It's jump 'er yer life!"

Richard hesitated. Not only was he afraid of heights, but leaping across a deep pit wasn't his favorite thing to do either! But the decision was made for him. The squid flung Richard and the ladder across the aisle, slamming him face first into a wall of books.

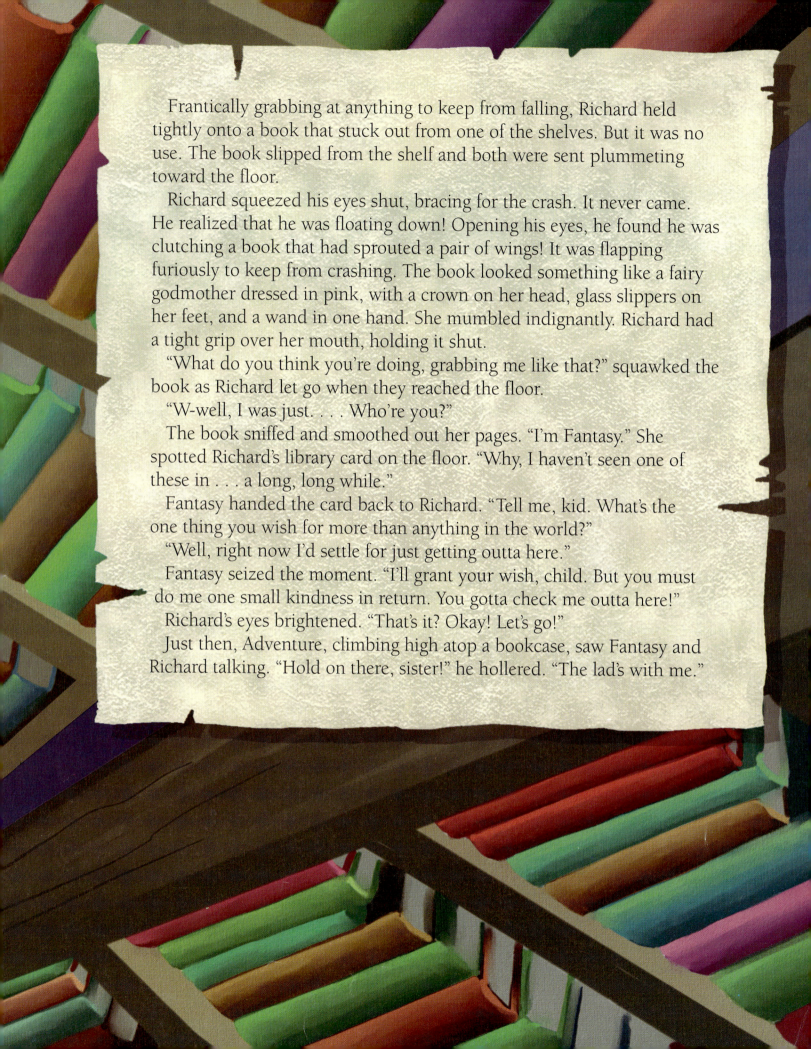

Frantically grabbing at anything to keep from falling, Richard held tightly onto a book that stuck out from one of the shelves. But it was no use. The book slipped from the shelf and both were sent plummeting toward the floor.

Richard squeezed his eyes shut, bracing for the crash. It never came. He realized that he was floating down! Opening his eyes, he found he was clutching a book that had sprouted a pair of wings! It was flapping furiously to keep from crashing. The book looked something like a fairy godmother dressed in pink, with a crown on her head, glass slippers on her feet, and a wand in one hand. She mumbled indignantly. Richard had a tight grip over her mouth, holding it shut.

"What do you think you're doing, grabbing me like that?" squawked the book as Richard let go when they reached the floor.

"W-well, I was just. . . . Who're you?"

The book sniffed and smoothed out her pages. "I'm Fantasy." She spotted Richard's library card on the floor. "Why, I haven't seen one of these in . . . a long, long while."

Fantasy handed the card back to Richard. "Tell me, kid. What's the one thing you wish for more than anything in the world?"

"Well, right now I'd settle for just getting outta here."

Fantasy seized the moment. "I'll grant your wish, child. But you must do me one small kindness in return. You gotta check me outta here!"

Richard's eyes brightened. "That's it? Okay! Let's go!"

Just then, Adventure, climbing high atop a bookcase, saw Fantasy and Richard talking. "Hold on there, sister!" he hollered. "The lad's with me."

"You know that short story?" asked Fantasy.

"Yeah. He's Adventure," said Richard.

Fantasy rolled her eyes. "Honey, that's what they all say."

Adventure began to fume and sputter. The two argued until the pirate book slipped and fell from the bookcase.

Richard turned to Fantasy. "Do something!"

Fantasy flicked her wand at Adventure, but forgot that its magic didn't work outside the Fantasy section. **SPLAT!** Adventure landed on the floor.

Richard ran over and helped the swashbuckler up. He looked up at Fantasy. "You mean you *can't* wish us to the exit?"

"I'd bet Flint's gold she's never even seen the exit," grumbled Adventure.

"More than you, shorty. In fact, the exit's just beyond my Fantasy section. I see it all the time from Rapunzel's tower."

"Then what're ye doin' in these parts?" Adventure shot back. "There's a witches' convention 'round here, maybe?"

The two books seemed to be having an age-old argument. "I've been misshelved," sniffed Fantasy. "But now young Prince Charming has come to check me out."

"My good eye he is!" shouted Adventure, pulling Richard away. "The lad's checkin' *me* out."

The two bickering books grabbed Richard's arms and pulled him in opposite directions. Fantasy tugged at Richard, saying, "Let's leave him. He doesn't even know where we are now!"

"Bilge water!" yelled Adventure. "Of course I know where we are." He reached up and pulled a book from the shelf, *The Hound of The Baskervilles*. Looking at the cover, he said, "We're in Baskervilles. Have a look see."

He handed the book to Richard, who innocently opened it. Suddenly a mangy, oversized hound dog leaped from the pages of the book. Fantasy quickly led them through an opening between some books on a shelf, but it was a dead end.

Richard groped for another opening along the shelves. His hand grasped a book that clicked and sent the entire bookshelf spinning around into a different aisle. They were safe!

Or were they? Once their eyes had adjusted to the darkness, they found themselves at the entrance to a dark and eerie graveyard.

A full moon cast a gray light over everything. Chills ran up Richard's spine. He had never been in a graveyard at night before.

"The Horror section," announced Adventure, drawing his sword. "Jest stick close to me and ye got nothin' to worry about."

Richard spotted the green EXIT sign through the fog. "There it is! Come on, we made it!"

Richard didn't see the creepy old haunted house between them and the exit. Nor did he hear the waves crashing below. "Looks like the only way to reach the exit is through that thar house," said Adventure.

Richard looked horrified. "No way I'm goin' in there!"

But it was their only chance to get out, so the threesome cautiously made their way toward the creaky iron gate. Headstones were scattered everywhere. Only they weren't made of stone, they were books. When the group reached the front door, Adventure told Richard to pull the dangling rope that hung from the belfry.

With trembling hands, Richard yanked the rope.

Suddenly, a hideous, misshapen book fell out of the tower and landed in front of them. They screamed. It screamed. The little book was Horror.

"Stand back, boy!" shouted Adventure, pointing his sword at the trembling lump of pages. "I'll give this hunchbook a taste of adventure."

Horror screamed and scurried back up the rope. "Sanctuary! Sanctuary!"

"Put that thing away," Fantasy called to Adventure. "You're frightening him." She flew up after Horror. "Come out, come out, wherever you are."

The terrified hunchbook thought they were frightened of the way he looked.

But Fantasy convinced him that they weren't. So he came out, but slipped and fell—right into Richard's arms.

"Good catch," said Fantasy, fluttering down next to Richard.

"Here, take it!" Richard yelped, tossing Horror back to Fantasy.

The poor hunchbook covered his face with his hands. "I know why you screamed. . . . It's because I'm . . . I'm h-horrible. I scared you."

"You mustn't judge a book by its cover," Fantasy told Richard.

"Let's start navigatin' this house," Adventure barked.

Horror cried, "Don't go in there! It's scary inside!" He turned to Richard. "I-I'm afraid."

Richard was curious. "Of what?"

"Of everything. Horror always has sad endings," the little hunchbook said.

"I come from a world of happy endings," Fantasy said. "Why don't you come with us?"

Richard, glad at last to be meeting someone who was as fearful as he was, assured Horror that they could use his help to get through the house. He took Horror's hand. Then he peered at the dark, shadowy entrance and slowly pushed the door open.

The others followed closely behind. They found themselves in a large, creepy, dark room with only a glimmering of light here and there. Rats and spiders seemed to be the only things living in the house. Richard called out to see if anyone else was at home. A raven swooped down over their heads. "Nevermore," it cawed.

Everyone scattered. From the shadows came a voice, "May I assist you in some way?"

Adventure drew his sword, ready to do battle. When the figure stepped forward they could see it was only a mild-looking, middle-aged man. Fantasy was intrigued.

"Oh, hello there, Mr. . . . ?"

"Doctor," said the man. "Doctor Jekyll."

"Well, sir, we did ring the bell . . ." Richard began.

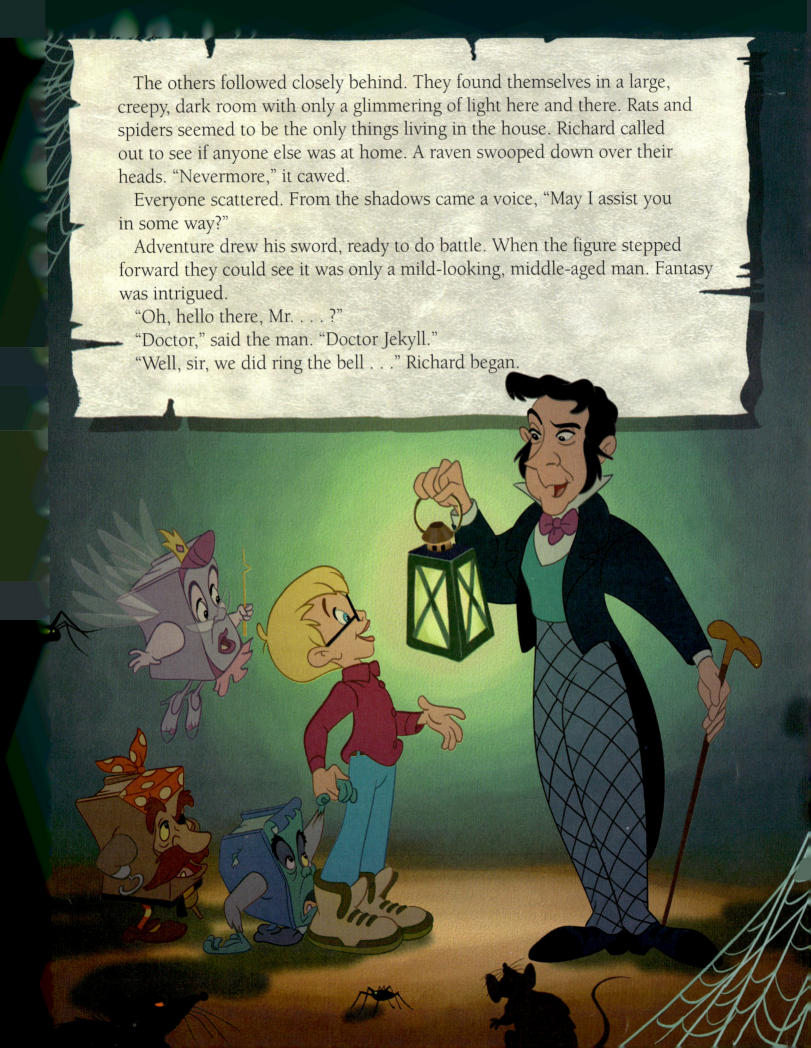

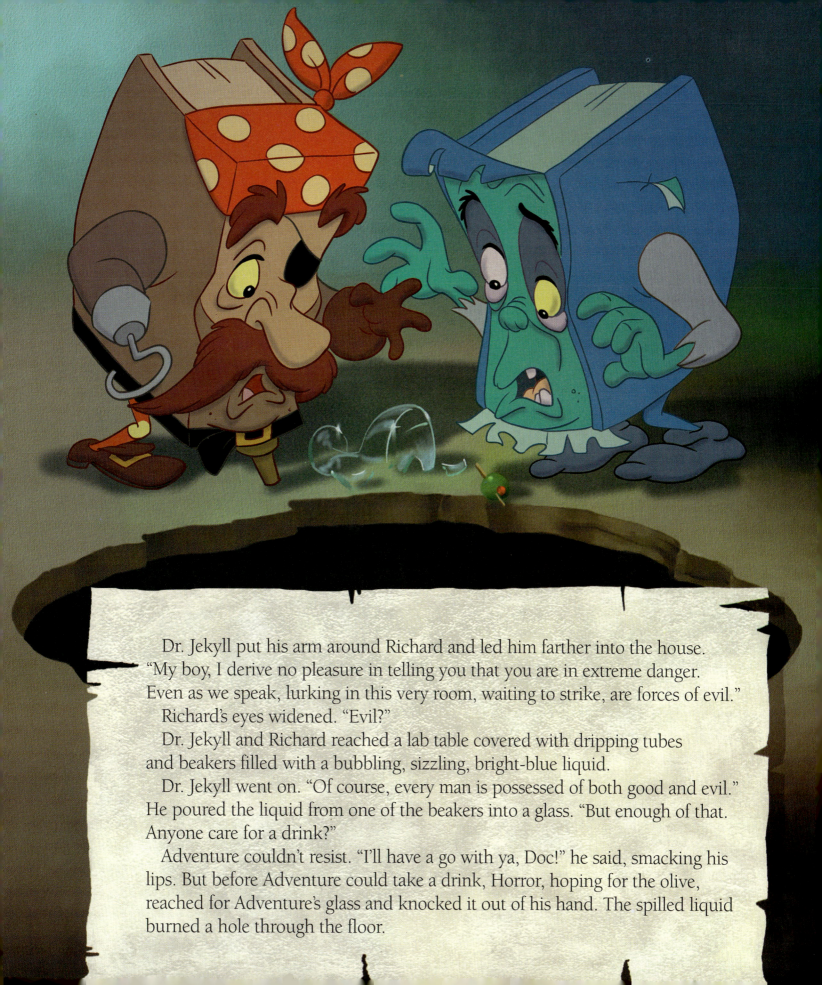

Dr. Jekyll put his arm around Richard and led him farther into the house. "My boy, I derive no pleasure in telling you that you are in extreme danger. Even as we speak, lurking in this very room, waiting to strike, are forces of evil."

Richard's eyes widened. "Evil?"

Dr. Jekyll and Richard reached a lab table covered with dripping tubes and beakers filled with a bubbling, sizzling, bright-blue liquid.

Dr. Jekyll went on. "Of course, every man is possessed of both good and evil." He poured the liquid from one of the beakers into a glass. "But enough of that. Anyone care for a drink?"

Adventure couldn't resist. "I'll have a go with ya, Doc!" he said, smacking his lips. But before Adventure could take a drink, Horror, hoping for the olive, reached for Adventure's glass and knocked it out of his hand. The spilled liquid burned a hole through the floor.

Richard and the group watched in amazement as Dr. Jekyll swallowed his drink. Then, clutching his throat, he let out a cry and began transforming into a hairy, disfigured creature.

"Doctor Jekyll?" Fantasy asked doubtfully.

"No! My name is Mr. Hyde! And no one leaves here alive!"

Terrified, Horror leaped up onto the chandelier. But it broke loose from his weight and crashed to the floor, causing Mr. Hyde to stumble backward into the hole in the floor. He grabbed at the chandelier to stop his fall, trapping Horror in its chains!

Adventure, not noticing Horror's predicament, pointed. "The stairs, mateys!"

"Help, Master," cried Horror. "Don't leave me here! Sanctuary! Sanctuary!"

The chandelier was sliding closer and closer toward the hole, while Mr. Hyde was straining to climb up the chain. "You've got to help Horror!" Fantasy cried to Richard. But Richard was paralyzed with fear. There was nothing he could do!

Fantasy let out an impatient sigh and flew over to Horror. Using her wand like a crowbar, she managed to free the trembling hunchbook. The chandelier disappeared down the hole, taking the screaming Mr. Hyde with it.

Horror ran over to Richard, who looked ashamed and embarrassed.

"It's okay, Master," said Horror, taking Richard's hand.

"I'da been twice as scared!"

As they climbed the stairs, Richard reached out to touch the stone wall. But instead, his hand passed right through a row of translucent books! Suddenly, moans, groans, and the sound of clanking chains began to fill the air.

"What's going on?" Richard asked Horror.

"Ghost stories!" cried Horror, trembling.

A host of wailing and screaming ghosts came flying out from the books.

Richard and the three books hurried past the ghost stories. Reaching a landing at the top of the stairs, they found four doors. Adventure looked at Horror. "Well, which one?"

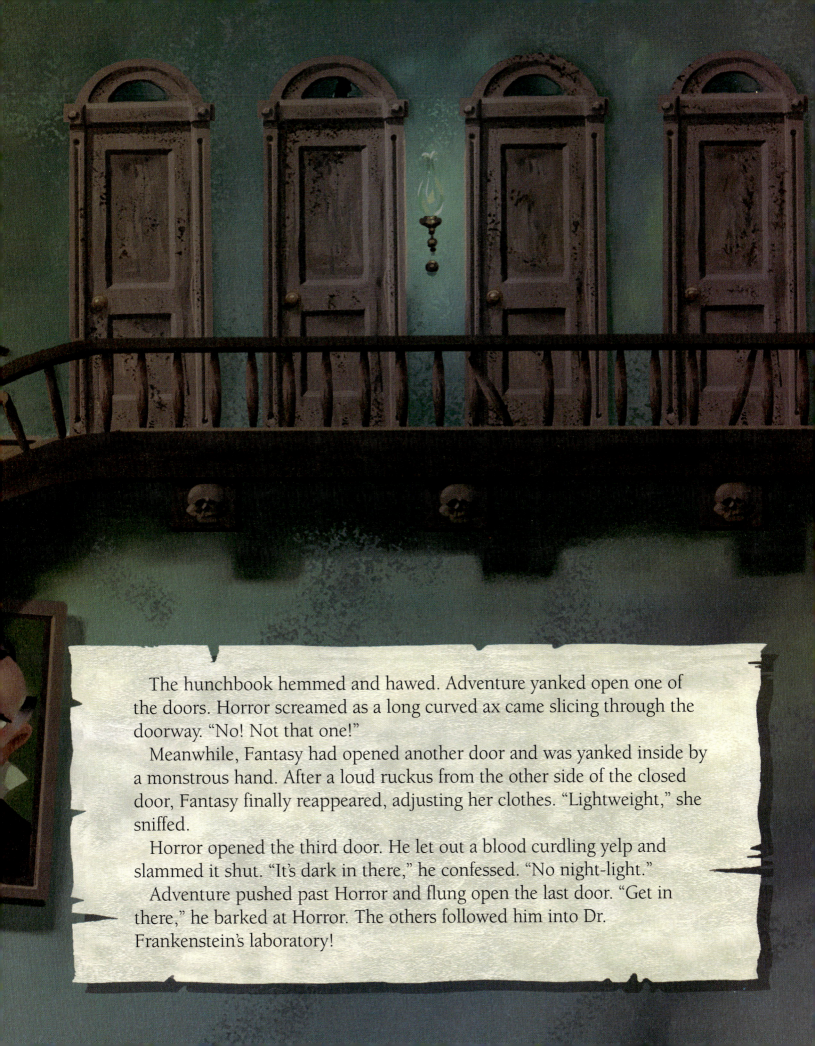

The hunchbook hemmed and hawed. Adventure yanked open one of the doors. Horror screamed as a long curved ax came slicing through the doorway. "No! Not that one!"

Meanwhile, Fantasy had opened another door and was yanked inside by a monstrous hand. After a loud ruckus from the other side of the closed door, Fantasy finally reappeared, adjusting her clothes. "Lightweight," she sniffed.

Horror opened the third door. He let out a blood curdling yelp and slammed it shut. "It's dark in there," he confessed. "No night-light."

Adventure pushed past Horror and flung open the last door. "Get in there," he barked at Horror. The others followed him into Dr. Frankenstein's laboratory!

The room was filled with bubbling beakers and steaming tubes coiling around glass bottles. If Richard and the books could just get past the draped slab in the center of the room, they would be on their way out. Fantasy noticed a trapdoor at the top of a long staircase. "Up there," she whispered to the others.

As they tiptoed past the slab, Frankenstein's monster sprang up from beneath the drapes. Screaming, the group dashed for the stairs, but the monster got there first. He caught Richard, who grabbed a rope that was dangling nearby.

Adventure looked up and saw that the rope was connected to a suspended platform near the ceiling. "Hold tight, matey," he called to Richard.

He slashed the rope with his sword just as Horror and Fantasy grabbed on. Richard and the three books were pulled up through a trapdoor as the platform fell to the floor.

The group was now on an observation deck in the tower. The only way to escape was down the dark side of the tower. Again, Richard froze in his tracks, listening to the waves crashing below.

"This way, mateys," called Adventure, as he jumped down onto an embankment. He looked up at Richard, who was peering down into the darkness. "Come on, boy! Even books have spines!"

BOOM! CRACK! The monster thrashed his way through the door. Horror scrambled toward the embankment, knocking over a cauldron of oil that spilled in front of the monster.

Fantasy seized a lighted torch from a nearby gargoyle and lit the oil. Instantly, there was a wall of fire between them and the monster. She flew over to Richard and pointed her wand over the embankment. "Move it!" she shouted.

Richard looked down. He looked back at the fire. He had to climb down. He just had to!

Richard started down the cliffside. Rocks crumbled under his feet and he began to slip.

"The vine, boy!" shouted Adventure. "Grab the vine!"

Richard saw it clinging to the stone wall. As he grabbed the vine, it snapped, plunging him toward the waves below.

But instead of being swallowed by the waves, Richard landed on a ledge with his friends. He had made it! He was all right!

Adventure leaned out over the edge and sniffed the salt air. "Do ye smell it?" he asked. "Breathe it in, mateys."

Before them the sun rose over a vast and shimmering ocean. The EXIT sign reappeared in the distance, then disappeared as the sun got brighter.

Adventure pointed his sword toward the ocean. "The Land of Adventure!" he said proudly.

EXIT

Richard and the books crawled over rocks, waded through waves, and ended up in a small cove. There, looking as if it were waiting just for them, was a small skiff. "C'mon, ya lubbers!" yelled Adventure. "Climb aboard!"

Richard looked at the boat suspiciously. "Is it safe?" Adventure assured him that it was as sturdy a vessel as had ever sailed the seas. But as he stomped about the boat, he drove his peg leg right through the bottom, and water immediately began to gush in. This time, Richard came to the rescue. He stuffed his handkerchief into the hole and stopped the leak.

"Shove off, lads," Adventure called to his crew of three. The small boat headed out to sea.

Before long a heavy fog rolled in and the sea began to swell, higher and higher.

"Geez, the water is getting kinda choppy," said Richard, becoming quite concerned as the boat was tossed roughly back and forth. "Maybe we should have stayed back where it was safe."

"Lad, a ship in port is safe, but that's not what ships were made for."

As the fog cleared a little, they could see that there were four other boats on the water. In the lead boat was none other than Captain Ahab, searching for the great white whale, Moby Dick.

"Thar she blows!" shouted Ahab, pointing at an enormous whale bursting through the water in front of them. "I grin at thee, thou grinning whale!"

Richard and the books watched with awe as the giant whale headed straight for Ahab's boats. After smashing into the whalers, Moby Dick turned toward them, mouth open wide, ready to devour the little boat.

"Abandon ship!" screamed Adventure.

Everyone dove into the water. Richard managed to grab onto a barrel and immediately popped up to the surface, sputtering and gasping. He looked around. There was no one in sight. "Guys?" he called out weakly. "Where are youuu?!" There was no reply, only silence.

Richard climbed atop some wooden planks that made a good raft. Then something blasted up through the water. It was Adventure! "Boy, am I ever glad to see you," said Richard.

Coughing, Adventure let Richard help him onto the planks. Richard couldn't resist hugging the soggy book. Embarrassed, Adventure pulled away.

"Where's Horror and Fantasy?" asked Richard.

Adventure looked out at the sea. "I searched for 'em much as I could, mate. 'Fraid they've gone below with Davey Jones."

Richard refused to believe his friends were gone. He called out for them, but there was no answer.

Then, seeing something circling their little raft, Richard cried out. "Sharks!"

Just when they thought they were goners, another boat appeared out of the fog. Richard waved frantically at the sailors, crying, "Help! Over here!"

"Careful, mate," said Adventure, as he eyed the boat. "Not all sharks are in the water."

The boat pulled up beside them. "It's a good thing you guys came along. We're missing two others about his size," said Richard, pointing to Adventure. "Have you seen them?"

The sailors curled their lips in mostly toothless grins. "The only catch we've had today is the two of ye."

From out of the fog an enormous Spanish galleon appeared, with the flag of the Jolly Roger atop its mast.

Richard and Adventure looked at each other and gulped. Pirates!

"I knew it!" said Adventure. "It's him. The meanest black-hearted pirate that ever sailed the seven seas—Long John Silver."

The grimy sailors let out a belly laugh and tossed Richard onto the deck of the pirate ship. Adventure reached for his sword, but the pirates pulled out their guns, ready for a fight. Richard's mouth went dry. Long John Silver ordered the pirates to stow their weapons. Richard's heart was pounding!

What were they going to do to him?

Adventure's voice cut through the thick air. "John Silver! Touch one hair on the boy's head and you'll be answerin' to me!"

The legendary pirate looked over at the small book and grinned. A sailor threw Adventure on deck, and he struggled to his feet, grumbling.

Silver scowled. "Ye wouldn't happen to be goin' after me treasure, would ye now?"

"Ye ain't got any treasure worth goin' after," said Adventure defiantly.

The pirates murmured uneasily. "He's lyin'!" shouted Silver. "There's plenty of treasure fer all of ye'! Search 'im. The boy, too."

The men turned Adventure upside down and shook him. All sorts of old-fashioned weapons clanked to the floor. Then it was Richard's turn. All they found in his pockets were the nail and the five-dollar bill his father had given him, and his library card. Silver picked his teeth with the nail and tossed the rest of the booty overboard.

Richard and Adventure watched with dismay as the library card floated away.

The watchman in the crow's nest cried out, "Land ho!" He pointed to a skull-shaped island off in the distance.

"There she be, mateys," cried Long John Silver. "Treasure Island!"

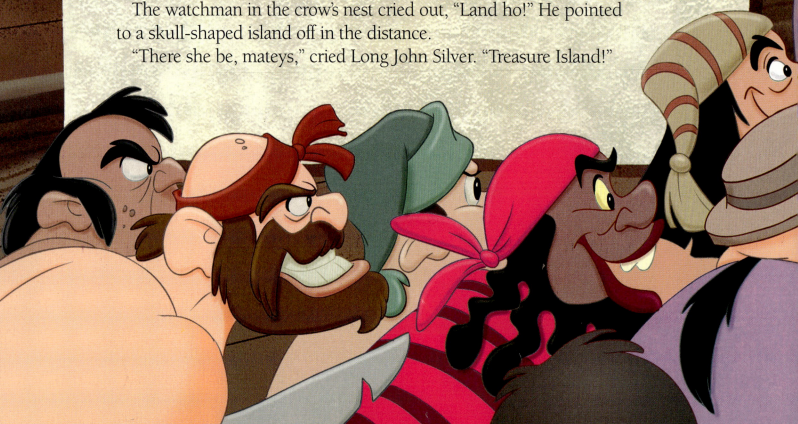

The pirates soon landed on the beach, dragging Richard and Adventure along by a rope.

"Stay on yer toes, mate," Adventure whispered to Richard. "When they go for the gold, we'll make our break."

The pirates followed their treasure map to the base of a tree. When they found the spot, they let out a howl. There, in an open pit, was a treasure chest, all right. But the treasure was gone!

Silver reached for his gun as the pirates closed in on him. "We mighta known you'd double-cross us," they snarled.

Just then a ghostly wail echoed from the treetops—and a pirate's song could be heard. "Fifteen men on a dead man's chest! Yo-ho-ho and a bottle of rum!"

The pirates turned toward the sound, pointing their weapons at the trees. "Evil spirits!" they shouted, shooting in all directions.

Then a horrible-looking lump attached to a rope came flying out of the treetops and slammed into the pirates, crying, "Sanctuary! Sanctuary!"

"Horror! You're alive!" cried Richard.

"Not for long," a pirate said, cocking his gun. But some fairy dust blew into his face causing him to sneeze and miss his shot.

Fantasy fluttered down to Richard, fairy dust trailing after her. "Fantasy!" cried Richard. Both his friends were safe!

The four friends soon ran the pirates off—all, that is, except Long John Silver.

Richard looked down and saw a pirate sword that lay between him and Silver. It was all up to him now, since Adventure had fallen into the treasure chest when the rope tying him to Richard was cut. Fantasy urged Richard to grab the sword.

"Don't even think it, boy," said Silver, moving toward the sword. "Ye ain't got the heart."

But Richard picked it up and pointed it right at Silver. "Stay back!"

Then the pirate spotted a skiff on the beach. "Yer not gonna make me get on that thar boat and sail away, are ye?"

"I-I'm not? . . . I mean, I am! That's exactly what I'm gonna do."

Richard knew that they would all be rid of the pirate if he did sail off. He ordered Silver to the boat, still pointing the heavy sword at him.

"Ye be a hard lad, Richard Tyler. Good sailin' to ye, shipmate," Silver said, climbing into the boat and rowing out to sea.

Fantasy and Horror crowded around Richard, cheering. "Wow! I wish my dad coulda seen me!" Then Richard said to his friends. "Boy, I thought you two were goners!"

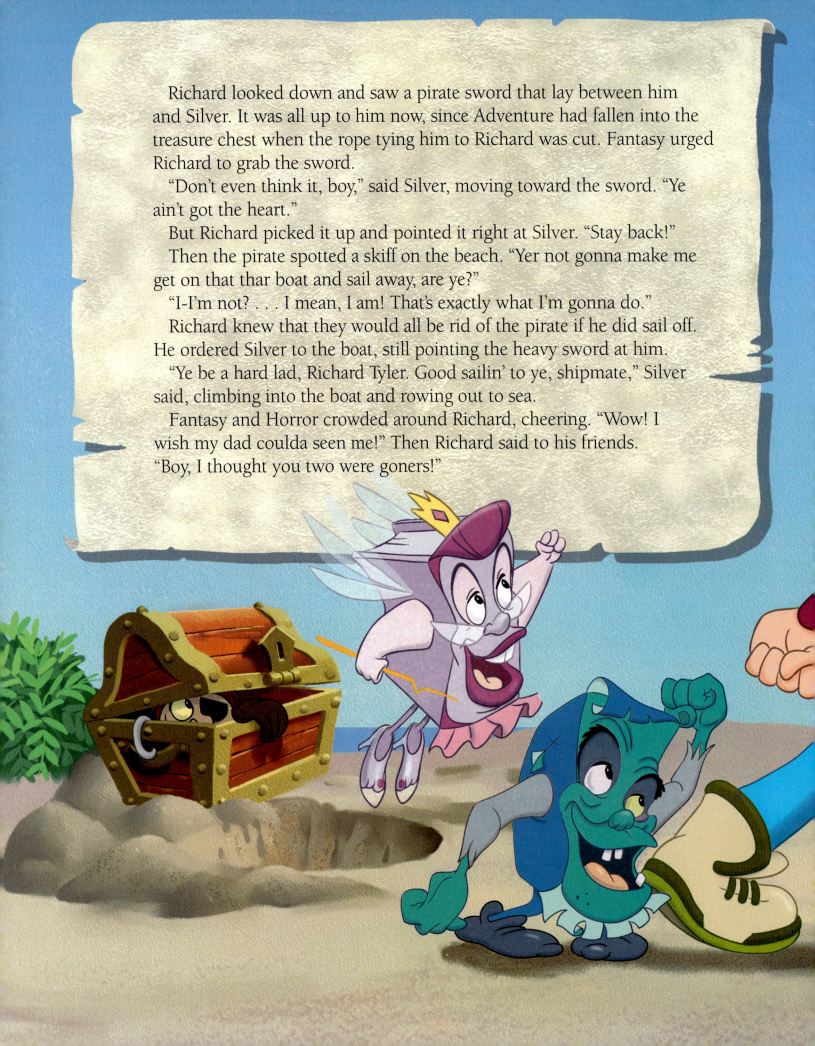

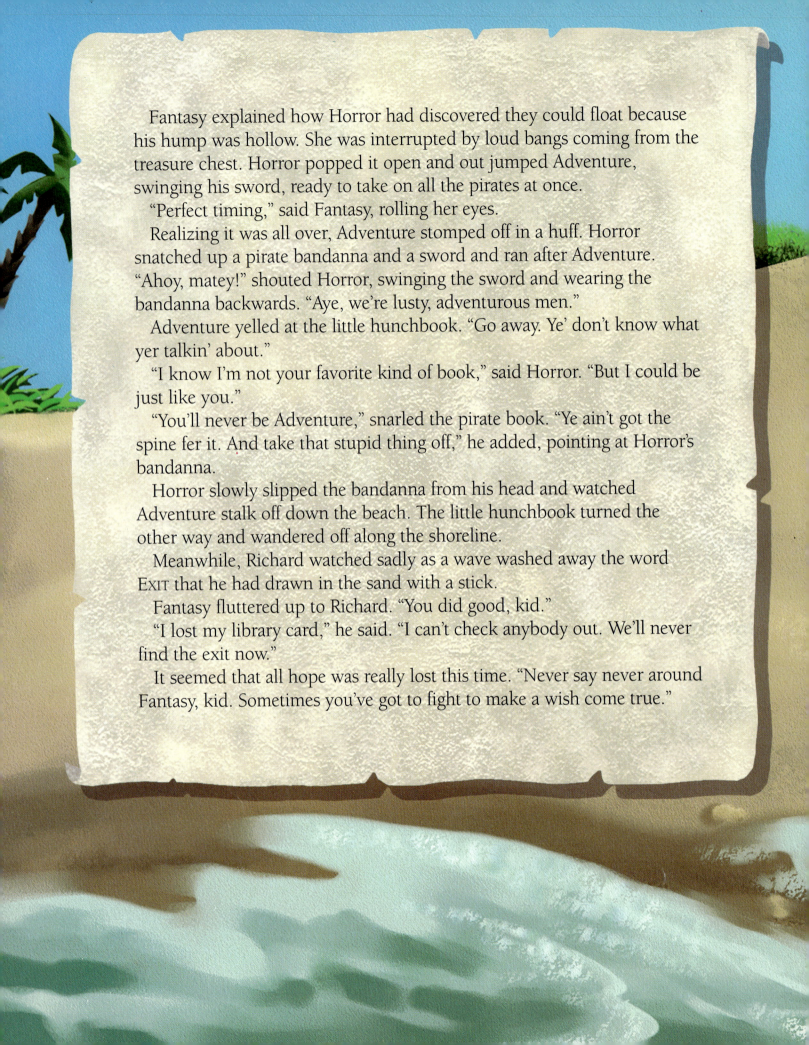

Fantasy explained how Horror had discovered they could float because his hump was hollow. She was interrupted by loud bangs coming from the treasure chest. Horror popped it open and out jumped Adventure, swinging his sword, ready to take on all the pirates at once.

"Perfect timing," said Fantasy, rolling her eyes.

Realizing it was all over, Adventure stomped off in a huff. Horror snatched up a pirate bandanna and a sword and ran after Adventure. "Ahoy, matey!" shouted Horror, swinging the sword and wearing the bandanna backwards. "Aye, we're lusty, adventurous men."

Adventure yelled at the little hunchbook. "Go away. Ye' don't know what yer talkin' about."

"I know I'm not your favorite kind of book," said Horror. "But I could be just like you."

"You'll never be Adventure," snarled the pirate book. "Ye ain't got the spine fer it. And take that stupid thing off," he added, pointing at Horror's bandanna.

Horror slowly slipped the bandanna from his head and watched Adventure stalk off down the beach. The little hunchbook turned the other way and wandered off along the shoreline.

Meanwhile, Richard watched sadly as a wave washed away the word EXIT that he had drawn in the sand with a stick.

Fantasy fluttered up to Richard. "You did good, kid."

"I lost my library card," he said. "I can't check anybody out. We'll never find the exit now."

It seemed that all hope was really lost this time. "Never say never around Fantasy, kid. Sometimes you've got to fight to make a wish come true."

Adventure came running up the beach. "Why're we sitting around like a bunch of old wenches at teatime?" he shouted, waving the library card in front of him. "Wrestled it away from three sharks, I did!" Adventure had really found the card stuck to his peg leg. It had been blown onto the beach by a gust of wind.

Richard perked up. "Where's Horror?"

Adventure looked down, ashamed at chasing the hunchbook away. "I'll go find him."

When he came upon Horror, Adventure was shocked. The motionless form of the hunchbook was tied down and surrounded by a mob of little people from *Gulliver's Travels* known as Lilliputians.

"Hang on, mate!" yelled Adventure. "I'm comin'!"

Bravely, Adventure faced the arrows of the Lilliputians. He cut the ropes just as Richard and Fantasy arrived. Embarrassed when Horror hugged him in thanks, Adventure pushed the hunchbook away. But Horror saw how much he really cared.

All at once, Fantasy's wand began blinking. "That can only mean one thing!" said Fantasy.

"The exit!" cried Richard.

"The check-out!" Adventure shouted.

"A happy ending!" sighed Horror.

"No, the Land of Fantasy," whispered Fantasy.

Her wand pointed away from the beach, leading them into a lush tropical forest. Adventure jumped ahead and began slicing a path through the thick bushes, leading the group deeper and deeper into the jungle. Gradually, the colors became brighter, the trees turned to gold, and the friends saw that the land was full of magical sprites.

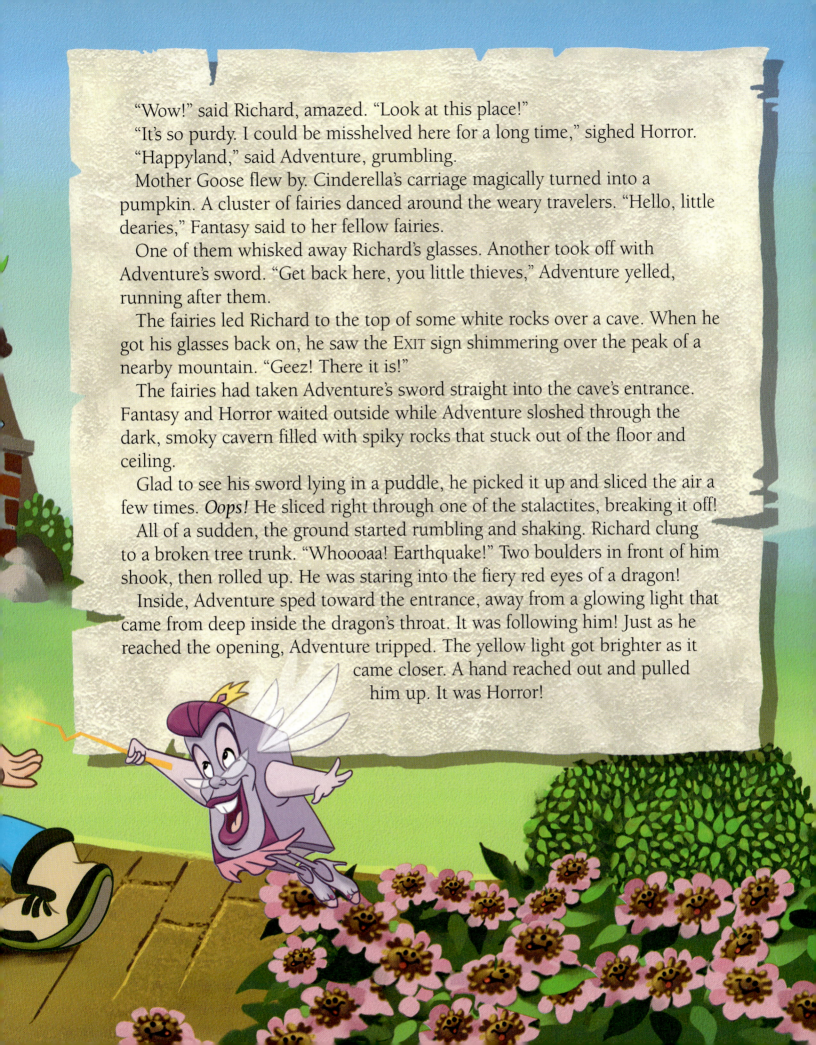

"Wow!" said Richard, amazed. "Look at this place!"

"It's so purdy. I could be misshelved here for a long time," sighed Horror.

"Happyland," said Adventure, grumbling.

Mother Goose flew by. Cinderella's carriage magically turned into a pumpkin. A cluster of fairies danced around the weary travelers. "Hello, little dearies," Fantasy said to her fellow fairies.

One of them whisked away Richard's glasses. Another took off with Adventure's sword. "Get back here, you little thieves," Adventure yelled, running after them.

The fairies led Richard to the top of some white rocks over a cave. When he got his glasses back on, he saw the EXIT sign shimmering over the peak of a nearby mountain. "Geez! There it is!"

The fairies had taken Adventure's sword straight into the cave's entrance. Fantasy and Horror waited outside while Adventure sloshed through the dark, smoky cavern filled with spiky rocks that stuck out of the floor and ceiling.

Glad to see his sword lying in a puddle, he picked it up and sliced the air a few times. *Oops!* He sliced right through one of the stalactites, breaking it off!

All of a sudden, the ground started rumbling and shaking. Richard clung to a broken tree trunk. "Whoooaa! Earthquake!" Two boulders in front of him shook, then rolled up. He was staring into the fiery red eyes of a dragon!

Inside, Adventure sped toward the entrance, away from a glowing light that came from deep inside the dragon's throat. It was following him! Just as he reached the opening, Adventure tripped. The yellow light got brighter as it came closer. A hand reached out and pulled him up. It was Horror!

The two books jumped off as the dragon rose up, a raging flame pouring up and out from the depths of its belly. Holding onto his tree, Richard was shaken from side to side as the dragon glared down on him. Fantasy turned to Horror. "Quick! Find page one thousand and one. *The Arabian Nights*."

Horror handed Fantasy the page. She tossed it in the air and then zapped it with her wand. It turned into a magic carpet. "Get the boy!" Fantasy said to the carpet.

Instantly, the carpet swooped down and whisked a screaming Richard up, up, up into the safety of the sky. Then it dove down to pick up the others and take them toward the exit.

On their way to the mountaintop, they flew past other creatures of a fantastical world: flying horses, flying camels, the genie from Aladdin's lamp, even other flying carpets. "We're gonna make it!" shouted Richard.

Horror couldn't hold back his excitement either. "Hooray! We're gonna make . . . *Oops!*" He knocked Fantasy's wand out of her hand and over the edge of the carpet!

Richard and the books watched the wand float down through the sky. Then the dragon's mouth burst through the clouds, and snatched the wand, swallowing it in one fierce gulp. This caused the dragon to cough up a fireball that sent the carpet careening into the mountainside. It crashed near the top, sending Richard and the books tumbling onto a ledge.

Shaking himself off, Richard knew he could still make it to the exit. He began climbing.

Richard continued his climb, unaware of the danger his friends were in. "We're almost there!" he cried, panting. He could practically touch the Exit sign. "We made it! C'mon!" he shouted to the others.

He spun around. They weren't there! He looked down the mountain and saw Adventure preparing to take on the dragon. The fiery beast had the books trapped inside a crevice. The dragon reared back, ready to release a blast of fire on Richard's friends. "Adventure!" yelled Richard. "Look out!"

Too late! Flames shot out from the dragon's mouth. Smoke filled the crevice. Fantasy and Horror tried to fan it away. Adventure passed out, his pages charred, his mustache smoldering. Richard looked down at his friends, who were facing certain doom. He looked up at the Exit sign. He could make it on his own! He could be safely at home, protected by his parents, in a matter of minutes. He could break his promise to his friends.

A faint cry came up from below. "Help, Master!" It was Horror. "Sanctuary! Sanctuary!"

Richard stopped for a moment. He had come so far. He had been through so much. Even his father would be proud. He really would. Richard spun around. "Hang on, guys! I'm coming!"

With renewed hope, Richard quickly climbed down the mountain to the crevice. He stopped on the way to pick up a sword, shield, and helmet from a long-dead warrior lying on the ground. He raced toward the dragon, aiming for its soft underbelly. The books cheered him on, offering warnings and advice: "Go fer the gizzard!" "Watch out for his tail!" "Bite 'im! Bite 'im!"

Richard raised his sword. Out of nowhere came the dragon's tail, swooping Richard up and whipping him right into the creature's mouth! Richard tumbled down, down into the slimy, grumbling pit of the beast's stomach. "I gotta get outta here," said Richard.

He found Fantasy's wand and tried it. It didn't work. He scrambled farther up, slipping on a pile of books. One fell on his chest. He remembered the words of the Pagemaster: "Look to the books."

Richard rummaged through the pile of books until he found just the right one—*Jack and the Beanstalk*. He ripped out the page he wanted and threw it down. A rumble arose. Then a thick beanstalk blasted up from the page, growing and coiling rapidly through the dragon's throat. Richard hopped on as it shot out of the dragon's mouth.

Fantasy, Horror, and Adventure watched in amazement as the dragon wrestled with the soaring beanstalk that carried Richard up and out of it's belly. As it shot past them, they all managed to jump on. When they reached the top of the mountain, Richard shouted, "Jump! Jump!" Just as the dragon's jaws snapped the beanstalk in two, they all let go, landing beneath the EXIT sign.

"Master, you saved us," cried Horror.

"That you did, matey," said Adventure.

Richard handed Fantasy her wand. "My hero!" she sighed, giving him a big hug.

They all turned toward the EXIT sign and entered through the double doors of a dome-shaped observatory. Inside, they watched respectfully as the Pagemaster emerged from the shadows. The books bowed and curtsied.

But Richard was angry. "Do you have any idea what I've been through? I was nearly torn apart by a madman, chased by a monster, and captured by pirates. Not to mention swallowed by a dragon!"

Fantasy bowed low. "Forgive him, Pagemaster."

"Nonsense! The boy is right," said the Pagemaster. "I purposely sent him through the Fiction section."

Richard smiled grimly. "Then you admit it."

"Of course," said the Pagemaster. "Think, boy! What kind of adventure would you have had if I'd brought you here with a turn of the page?"

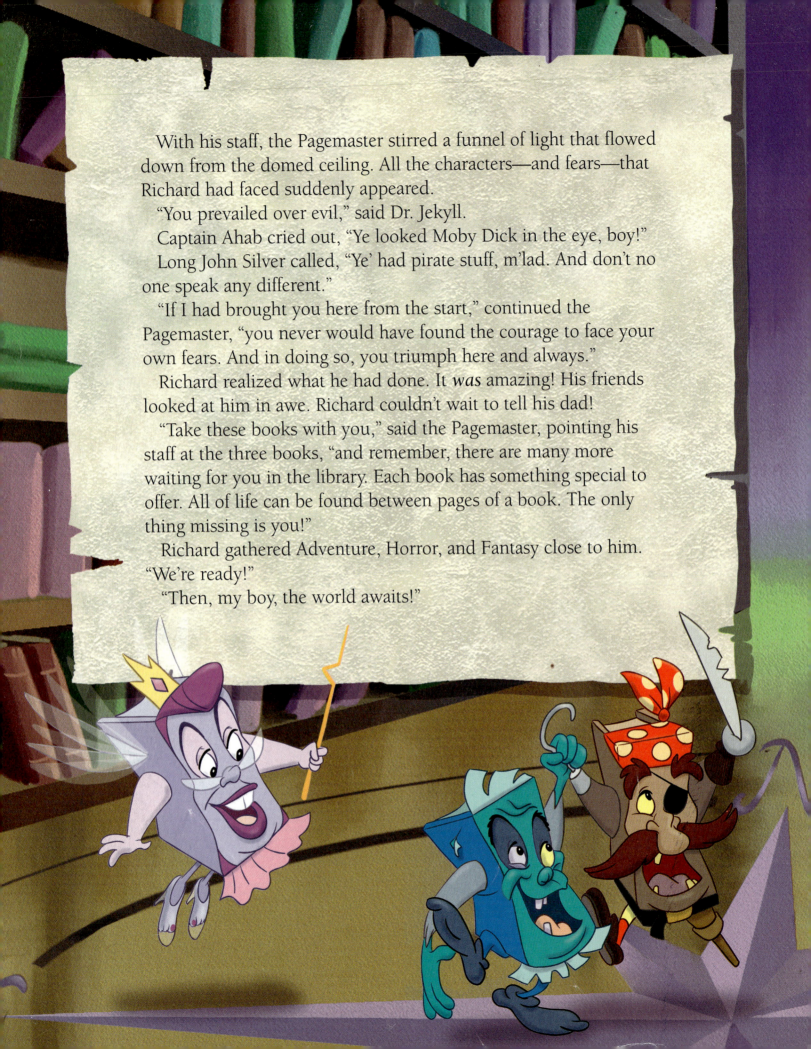

With his staff, the Pagemaster stirred a funnel of light that flowed down from the domed ceiling. All the characters—and fears—that Richard had faced suddenly appeared.

"You prevailed over evil," said Dr. Jekyll.

Captain Ahab cried out, "Ye looked Moby Dick in the eye, boy!"

Long John Silver called, "Ye' had pirate stuff, m'lad. And don't no one speak any different."

"If I had brought you here from the start," continued the Pagemaster, "you never would have found the courage to face your own fears. And in doing so, you triumph here and always."

Richard realized what he had done. It *was* amazing! His friends looked at him in awe. Richard couldn't wait to tell his dad!

"Take these books with you," said the Pagemaster, pointing his staff at the three books, "and remember, there are many more waiting for you in the library. Each book has something special to offer. All of life can be found between pages of a book. The only thing missing is you!"

Richard gathered Adventure, Horror, and Fantasy close to him. "We're ready!"

"Then, my boy, the world awaits!"